Timotl

Dog Knows Best

Dog Knows Best

By

Timothy Glass

As told by

Panda the Beagle

Table of Contents

Other Books by Timothy Glass

Nonfiction

Just This Side of Heaven

Fiction

Postcards

Sleepytown Beagles, Doggone It

Sleepytown Beagles, In The Doghouse

Children's Fiction

Sleepytown Beagles, Panda Meets Ms. Daisy Bloom

Sleepytown Beagles, Penny's 4th of July

Sleepytown Beagles, Oh Brother

Sleepytown Beagles, Differences

Sleepytown Beagles, The Lemonade Stand

Sleepytown Beagles, Jingle Beagles

Sleepytown Beagles, Up, Up and Away

Cover design by Timothy Glass
Photo on back cover and bio by Kim Jew
Photo of Panda Glass, front cover by Timothy Glass
Library of Congress control number: 2017964742
ISBN:978-0-9984121-6-0
Printed in the USA

Dedication

To Elise: Your laughter and smile were contagious, and your life was way too short. Until we meet again, all my love, Dad.

To Panda: Thank you for all the wonderful memories, your unconditional love, and all the fun we had together.

on the human race—a guideline, if you will, for humans to name their best friends. However, we pups have our paws full with much more difficult issues than whether or not to name a 180-pound rottweiler "Baby" or "Sissy" or to call a chihuahua "Rocky" or "Rambo."

Yes, the task of understanding and training your human is a daunting challenge, at best. Nevertheless, I do possess a higher understanding of human beings and their needs, and I can help. Oh yes, humans do require lots of understanding, God love them! It is a good thing we canines are around to provide that, as well as unconditional love. So, wipe off your paws, curl up on the couch next to your human, and allow me to explain so you can better understand your human. With any luck, they, too, will read this book.

Home Is Where the Dog Is

THE WORD "HOME" MAKES many people picture a tranquil setting: a cozy living room with a blazing fire in the fireplace and a man reading a newspaper in his slippers, a canine curled up at his feet. Sounds like a scene taken straight from a Norman Rockwell painting, doesn't it? Wrong!

Needless to say, humans seem to have many issues related to the house. First, for the record, I would like to point out that our human counterparts simply do not get it. The house is ours! As is the sidewalk that surrounds the house, the mailbox, and the most cherished thing of all, what they call a trashcan. The trashcan is another classic example of humans' misinterpretation and inability to truly comprehend the significance of something so important to us dogs. The "trashcan" is actually the treasure box. Both inside and outside of the house, this box contains a treasure trove of smells and objects as well as a great smorgasbord of tasty treats any canine would be more than willing to dine on. However, in all my years, I have never once seen a human feast on its savory, decadent contents. In fact, in my extensive research of human behavior, I have noticed the large treasure box on the outside of the house left carelessly at the curbside each week.

While most humans don't grasp the true meaning behind the treasure box, certain highly intelligent humans do. We pups call these individuals the treasure box hunters! Ever notice that when your human leaves the treasure box out at the curb, it attracts humans who drive by in large, noisy trucks and pick up the contents? This is only a theory at this point—speculation, if you will. Nevertheless, I can assure you there is widespread, ongoing research as to how this select group of highly intelligent humans knows exactly when and where a treasure box has been haphazardly left by the curbside. I speculate they not only have a higher intelligence than most humans do, but also possess a keener sense of smell, similar to that of us canines. The treasure box hunters are cunning as well. They always use a noisy truck to distract our humans when we bark frantically to alert them that someone is, in fact, stealing the contents of our treasure box. Alas, this is not the only inadequacy of our humans. Let's look at some other classic examples.

Have you ever noticed the younger single human breeds? I like to refer to them as strays. Once they slip their leash, they just can't seem to remember where they live unless they have a pup to come home to. Without a canine, they have been known to stay out all hours of the night, wandering about, God only knows where. That is where the canine counterpart comes into play. We provide a much-needed balance in this equation. Thus, every home should have 2.4 dogs. In fact, I firmly believe the realtor-type breed of human should provide a dog for every dog-less home. Think of the marketing strategy: quaint country home with three bedrooms, two bathrooms, on a quarter of an acre, with a collie. Ah…now, that is truly home sweet home.

The next issue about the home I would like to address is humans' crazy obsession with cleaning the carpet and furniture. I have found most humans have absolutely no clue how hard we canines work to get just the right combination of dog hair and scent into the carpet. We do all this work only to have them drag out that mechanical noisemaker on wheels, which is capable of sucking up a shih-tzu from a quarter of a mile away, and destroy the beautiful aroma. Removal of the dog hair on the furniture is my next pet peeve. H-E-L-L-O, it is we, your canine companions, who put the "fur" in the word "furniture." Duh! Why on earth do you think it was named that?

Another issue that our poor humans don't seem capable of wrapping their brains around is the yard. That's right, the great outdoors. Most pups, myself included, will tolerate a lot. Take, for example, what your human calls "patio furniture," scattered haphazardly around the yard. I have watched my human dad and mom come home with the latest Home Depot collection, place things around the backyard, and stand back with pleased smiles. However, I'd like to see them, just one time, blast through the backyard to bark at the postman. If we canines needed an agility course, we'd ask for one. Needless to say, we pups put up with it.

There is another thing I think humans are totally missing about the backyard: that moist, dark, cool soil that has been put around the outermost edges. Once again, communication is key here. Does the human ask us first before planting a daisy or rose bush? No! Or as they would say to us, "No, Fluffy, no, no!" What my human does, and I am sure yours as well, is stray from the house. Once they finally pick up their scent—which, I might add, is quite a challenge for most humans—they return with a trunk-load of potted plants. Next, the human will begin what I call their potting ritual. Oh yes, the human breed has a potting ritual that dates back to the early 1500s. The ritual commences with the human walking back and forth, holding a helpless plant by the stem, scouting out prime real estate and plopping in a rose here and a carnation there, usually in the moist, dark, cool soil I've mentioned. If we canines required all this plant life surrounding us, don't you think for a minute we would live in a jungle? Good grief! Once again, the humans have no clue.

Anyway, back to what I was explaining. What your human calls a flowerbed is really a beagle bed, in my case, or a basset bed or a collie bed. You get my meaning. It is the one and only ergonomically created dog bed on this earth. (Mind you, I think there is a real market out there if any of you pups would like to create a real dictionary for humans to use.) Maybe then the humans might understand. It is no wonder we pups have our paws full of dirt, digging out that

extensive research into human and canine behavior has shown that daylight saving time has caused more confusion between our human counterparts and us than anything else. I have to paw it to them, as they did come up with some cutesy little phrases. In autumn, we are to fall back and in the springtime, we are to spring forward. Needless to say, that is the only redeemable quality of this stupid concept. Take, for example, the fall, when they say "fall back." My breakfast and dinner times are an hour later, as I am sure yours are. That's not to mention potty time, my walk, naptime, treats, and my bedtime. In the spring, we are to spring forward. You're doggone right we want to spring forward, duh! We canines are so thrilled to be back on track and to put this idiotic system of time behind us. For months, we keep our paws crossed that mankind will never again expect canines to endure this. However, as the leaves turn from green to shades of gold and then begin to fall, once again so does the time.

For the record, we are not the only ones confused by this time manipulation, oh no. Critters around the globe are quite confused by the absolute craziness. The sun and the moon did not get the memo, either. Have you ever tried to go to sleep when the sun is still beaming a ray of light through the bedroom drapes? I might as well be in the direct path of the Luxor Hotel in Las Vegas with its 40-billion-candlepower sky beam aimed directly at my bed.

We pups need our beauty rest! And daylight saving time is not the only issue involving time that drives a wedge between us and our humans. Try traveling with your human from the East Coast to the West Coast or vice versa. Your stomach is on a highly calibrated canine clock that knows no time zone except its own. Go to Grandma's house on the West Coast for the week and now your dinnertime is three hours later. H-E-L-L-O, it simply does not work that way!

It is my expert opinion that canines have one of the most sophisticated measures of time on earth. Frankly, the human race could learn a thing or two from us.

Bath Time, Not!

AS I HAVE MENTIONED before, the human race seems obsessed with being clean. Why, I have no idea. I think it has to do with their challenges with scent. They simply have no idea what smells good. For example, the average human will, without the aid of a leash, willingly climb into one of those closets in the house that has a shiny chrome garden hose coming out of the wall. I think their term for it is a "shower." I have never been able to figure this one out. When it rains, humans will use a large circular item called an umbrella to keep themselves from getting wet. However, each day they go into the closet and turn the water on themselves, spending 10 to 15 minutes scrubbing away their scent.

When they come out, do they shake the water off like any sensible canine would do? No! They stand there, dripping water all over the tile floor. Most canines would at least lap that great-tasting water off the floor. Do humans? Once again, they are as clueless as a snow blower about proper water usage. In an attempt to dry their inferior fur, they'll use a towel. If you have a female human in your household, she will spend the same amount of time it took to build the Sistine Chapel fussing with the fur on top of her head. She will dry it with a handheld wind machine that sounds like a cat being de-clawed.

As a canine, I'll be the first to admit I love the wind blowing through my ears and my lips flapping in the breeze, with an occasional bug heading in my direction as a bonus. However, canines can achieve the same measure of pleasure simply by hanging their heads out the window of a moving car. Simple fun without getting wet or spending a dime. Nonetheless, my human mom uses the handheld wind machine.

Her next step is to fill the shower room – and any room within a five-mile radius – with a bombardment of smells, including lotions and perfumes that could have even the most stuffed-up pug coughing, wheezing, and sneezing for a week. To complete this daily ritual…oh yes, there is more. I like to refer to it as war paint; again, this is usually, but not always, limited to the female human. She will pull out jar after jar and tube after tube of what they call "makeup." By the time she is done, she will have applied enough war paint (or makeup) to cover an airport runway. Once finished, she looks and smells like, well, only a human could.

Nevertheless, many humans feel that, from time to time, we canines need what they call a bath. From humans' point of view, this can be accomplished only by first going to one of those places that sells everything a human thinks we canines need. They will spend two times the nation-al deficit on bottles, towels, and colorful containers filled with smelly items such as doggie shampoo and conditioner, to name just a few.

For the record, I'm venting here a little. I would like to say that the happy dogs pictured on any of those containers must be on drugs! Either that or the man-ufacturers use Velcro to stick their furry little butts on that tub! Let's face it; no normal red-blooded canine would ever sit still in a tub of that smelly stuff looking so doggone happy. Not all of you will be given a bath at home. Some of you will be lured into the car with the pretense of getting to go bye-bye. Wrong! You will be whisked away to some place called the Happy Dog Day Spa or the Tail Waggers Dog Wash. Trust me…been there, done that. I was not happy, nor was my tail wagging!

Bath time at our household begins with what I like to call the 500-meter sprint. Of course, that equates to "catch me if you can." Once I see my humans break out that nasty-smelling stuff, I usually decide that I have someplace I r-e-a-l-l-y need to be. It can be any place, just not that closet with the chrome garden hose.

When they catch me, I am doomed to sit in that closet for about the same amount of time it took the North and South to fight the Civil War. All the while they tell me I'll be okay. Really? By the time they are finished with me I'll smell like a perfume counter at Macy's, not like a dog! This is why I will back myself into a corner and try to protect every square inch of fur on which I still have scent. Let's face it; I have worked extremely hard to achieve this smell since the last time they did this to me.

After my fur has absorbed enough water to sink the Titanic, they let me out. The next step is one only a human could have invented, and that is to try to towel me off. Hey, why waste the time when the carpet – or, my favorite, their bed with the freshly cleaned sheets or comforter – is available to rub myself on? It works for me!

Communication Error

COMMUNICATION IS ONE OF my favorite topics to bark about. Needless to say, at times there seems to be some problems getting the message from point A to point B. In my case, I have a condition termed Beagle Selective Hearing. This condition is not limited to just the beagle, either, no sir! It can plague even the strongest rottweiler. It is a proven medical fact that many canines suffer from it. My extensive research has shown that almost 99.9% of us pups are stricken with this untreatable issue. I believe we get it from our humans. That's correct, from our humans! Hear me out on this one. You pups who live in a two-human household have probably witnessed the same issue I have. Take, for example, when my human mom says something to my human dad. My human dad, who has what is called Male Selective Hearing, is watching TV when my human mom comes into the room and tells him something. A few hours later she will state the very same thing and he has absolutely no clue what she is talking about.

With us canines, it works something like this. When I am dining on tasty treats out of the humans' trashcan, the words, "Panda, what are you doing?" fall into some large black vortex before actually getting to me. Beagle Selective Hearing is to blame.

Just the other day, that large brown truck driven by the man dressed in brown came rumbling down our street and passed our house. I know for a fact that this truck brings me things in cardboard boxes. Treats, collars, blankets, you name it. He must have forgotten to stop with my package, so I barked. My human counterpart proceeded to tell me something and all I heard was "blah, blah, blah." The same thing happens when someone rings my doorbell. Humans and canines have had this condition since my ancestors allowed the human race to live in the caves with them.

the backyard for an after-dinner chomp or two on the lawn, they would realize those tiny, scrumptious green blades help with digestion. In fact, they'd be adding a few extra minerals to their diet. They could then toss out half those tiny jars of medications and supplements cluttering up the cabinet to make more room for your kibble and treats!

Another thing to consider is the way they eat their food. Granted, I have my bowl, but I have no problem whatsoever eating off the floor. When my humans are preparing food in the room they call the kitchen, if I manage to place myself strategically underfoot, I can sometimes magically make food fall on the floor. With the speed of a NASCAR screaming down the track, I can grab, chew, and have it down the hatch and still have time to sit back and look innocent.

Oh, I almost forgot. My favorite is

when tiny humans show up at my house. You know, those miniature humans with wobbly legs who can go from laughing to a screaming fit in two-tenths of a nanosecond. For some reason, those tiny humans do not understand the concept of the food zone any better than their full-size counterparts do. Why, I can't understand, as it is a simple concept most pups understand. If it is within our reach, it is ours! Take, for example, when a little human wobbles over to you with a cookie in hand; any red-blooded canine knows where that cookie is going to end up. It is just a matter of logistics and seconds before you snatch that cookie. First, the cookie is within reach, so it is in the canine food zone. Next, these tiny humans have no grip strength whatsoever. Let's face it, in a match between a yorkie and the tiny human, my money is on the yorkie for sure.

My other favorite thing is when the

human sets his lunch or dinner on one of those small tables in the living room and then leaves. The canine will calculate the height of the table, quickly determining that the food is clearly within the food zone, and then it is gone. It amazes me, and I am sure any pup, when the human returns to the room and seems stunned that the food is gone. The most common thing to hear them say is, "What have you done?"

My thoughts exactly: What do you think? The food was in the food zone and I ate it. Duh.

The Drive-Through Window

WHILE I AM ON THE subject of eating, let me discuss the topic of the drive-through window. You canines, if you have not already done so, have to check this out. The biggest problem I can see is that it's too bad we canines can't drive to one ourselves. Canines call this the magic window.

Allow me to explain for those of you who have not been able to experience this first paw. Say you and your human are out for a drive. Were you aware that your human can pull over alongside certain buildings? Usually there is a long line of humans waiting to get to the magic window, and for good reason. They say we canines are pack-like creatures, but this display of human pack behavior leads me to believe that our humans also gather in packs.

Wonder what your human is up to, pulling up to a building with a magic window? Listen and observe; your human is waiting with the pack for a chance at the magic window. I am still extensively researching the pecking order of the human pack. What I am attempting to uncover is how I can change their system so that my human is the first one at the magic window while bypassing that large, colorful plastic box that talks to them. I might mention that the talking sign does only one thing: hurt my sensitive ears.

At any rate, the human finally manages to make it to the front of the line. When he does, the smells that come out of that window make me want to perfect the long jump across my human's lap, out of the car, and into the magic window so that I can help myself to all the food. I state this as a fact from experience.

Once the meal comes through that window, the drive back home takes about as long as it took the Mayflower to cross the Atlantic. All the while, I am forced to endure the tantalizing smells from the bags or boxes of food. For some reason, I assume that humans have an inferior ability to sniff out food, as the human does not seem bothered by the smells. Nonetheless, the human does show signs of being very territorial. For this reason, don't even attempt to sneak over and snatch the contents within those containers or the human will fight you for them.

Shed Happens

HOME IS WHERE THE dog hair is attached to just about everything, they say, except for "me," the dog. A dash of hair here and a clump of hair there is all part of making a house a home, right, pups? Beyond the simplest explanation as to why this happens, shedding is our artistic expression and part of the Canine Bill of Rights. What, you had no idea we have a Bill of Rights? Well, we do and the artistic right to shed is one of our amendments.

The Canine Bill of Rights was pawed by Lassie, Rin Tin Tin, Benji, Old Yeller, Scooby Doo, and Snoopy. But enough about canine history; allow me to get back to what I was saying. The proper placement of hair around the house, the car, and even your human's clothes is an art form. From puppyhood to full-grown adults, we canines are true artists and we perfect our art throughout our lifetimes. This is why I like to stand back after getting off the couch and admire my creation as though it's the next Rembrandt or Picasso. Knowing this is a work in progress, I diligently work on the masterpiece each and every day. That is, until my human comes along with that noise machine called a vacuum. The canines in our household have nicknamed that noise machine "Jaws." Once again, I only speculate that the ancestry of the vacuum is directly related to the wind machine my human mom uses to dry her hair. While the wind machine blows, the vacuum sucks things up. One thing is for sure – this thing the human calls a vacuum is capable of sucking up a shih-tzu from a mile away. I truly believe our humans have no eye or appreciation for art. Why else would they destroy all our hard work, I ask you? I can only assume this is why you can visit art galleries around the world, from France to the United States, and not see any of our ancestors' masterpieces hanging on the walls or sitting on display. It is "hair" today, gone tomorrow.

Nonetheless, we express unconditional love and understanding for our humans' behavior, and within an hour we will be back diligently working on our next masterpiece on the couch, the carpet, the car, or our humans' clothes. They are our canvases of choice.

Now, here's the thing. Our hair placement on the human's clothes goes far beyond just an art form, oh yes. Sit, stay, take notes, and don't roll over just yet. Have you ever been left alone while your human mom or dad leaves the house? I am sure you have. When they return, have you ever sniffed out the scent of another pup on them? You can spend literally hours sniffing to get your point across to your human, knowing they have strayed in your absence.

My favorite response from my human mom is, "Do you smell another puppy?"

Duh, is Snoopy a beagle? I have a finely tuned, highly trained nose that can detect bacon before it is even sliced. What do you think?

While I am not Dear Abby, Dr. Phil, or even Dr. Laura, allow me to give you some heart-to-heart advice, fur-kids. Hair placement on your human's clothes is vital. First and foremost, it sends a message to other canines that this human is taken. My human dad and mom wear what they call wedding rings. These rings show other female and male humans that my human mom and dad are taken. Therefore, what your hair does, along with stating that the human is taken, is create a "scentaddress" much like what the humans call an address. Oh yes, "scentaddress" is a real word.

Think of hair placement on your human as your commitment to them, a way of showing they are yours. You are only marking your territory. Furthermore, if they become lost, the "scentaddress" will return them to you.

While we are on the subject of canine artwork, my favorites are paw art and nose art. Allow me to clarify this for those of you who have not yet tried it. There is nothing quite as breathtaking as a muddy paw work of art. In fact, mud happens to be one of my favorite media to work with. Oh yes, while outside, I can collect enough mud on my paws to paint the complete Sears Tower. But, of course, any canine would be out of their mind to waste their talent on a building. My canvas of choice is the carpet; I rush through the open back door and head straight for it. Now pups, take it from the master, simple paw strokes are appealing but skid marks and swirls add so much depth and texture to your artwork. As I promised, this will be breath-taking for you as well as for your human. I have seen my own humans gasp for breath, at a loss for words when they stand back and admire my craft. I can only assume they are so amazed by this beautiful work of art before them that they simply can't speak. However, as I mentioned before, the carpet is just one thing you may want to try your paw at. Don't be afraid to expand your tal-ent to the couch and even their bed.

My next talent (yes, I am a multi-tal-ented gal) is that I have perfected my nose art skills to a master level. Pups, you have to try this, so let me explain just how and where to do this. You may use your boring, average, everyday sliding glass door or any door with glass within your reach. If you don't have any glass in your house within your reach, don't worry. You can usually climb on the back of a couch or chair and reach the windows. If so, that will work. Also, one of my all-time favorites is the window in the family car. Simply place your wet nose against the glass and create. In fact, in the family car I like to spread the art around from window to window. Remember, one stroke of the nose is not enough to add the depth and texture you need for a masterpiece. Really apply as much as you can. In my lifetime, I have created a complete collection of nose art any canine would be proud of.

Vet

AS YOU MAY HAVE already figured out, the vet's office is not the most popular place on earth for us fur-kids. In fact, I have been talking to Congress and legislating to pass the Anesthesia Act. You may ask yourself, "What is the Anesthesia Act?" The Anesthesia Act would require each veterinarian to administer anesthesia as we fur-kids enter a clinic. I don't care if the vet wants to trim my nails, I want anesthesia. Look into my ears? Anesthesia. In fact, I would like to sleep through any procedure the vet deems necessary.

Let us take a closer look into the so-called canine clinic. My well-meaning human once lured me into the clinic for what was called a routine checkup. Let me tell you, there is nothing routine about this. First, I was put on an ice-cold metal table (where, I might add, I sounded much like Sammy Davis Jr. tap dancing while trying to get my footing). Well, let's be honest here, I was trying to get off the table and out of that place. The metal table was so darn cold on my paws, the thing could have doubled as a freezer. In fact, I do believe that underneath the table I saw refrigerator coils plugged into electrical current...really!

Next, the veterinarian assistant (I am sure her name was Helga; I know I once saw her on TV with the World Wrestling Federation) put me into a headlock as the veterinarian looked into my ears. Did they think I took something from their waiting room and stuffed it into my ears? Then, just when you think the worst is over, it gets worse, my little furry friends. Next, they got out a Q-tip. It was the same length as the Golden Gate Bridge and, you guessed it, they stuck all 8,981 feet of it into my ears. Then they took a bottle (I am sure it was at least three gallons) and poured every last drop of its contents into both my ears. I was drenched; however, I do believe there was a method to their madness. This was to prevent me from hearing and understanding what they were explaining to my human. In fact, I do believe I could have stuck my entire head into the lobby fish tank and it would have sounded the same.

Next, the vet grabbed what she called a thermometer, which was about the same size as the Q-tip. Before I could say, "You're going to stick that where?" they stuck all 8,981 feet up my butt. I may not have a medical degree, but I have had a temperature before and never was it in my rear end. So, in a gazillion years no one has bothered to think up a better way to take a canine's temperature? Come on, folks! After that they poked a hole in my coat and gave me a shot. For all I had to endure on my trip to the vet clinic, I got a lousy metal tag to wear on my collar. The stupid thing didn't even have my name on it or come in my favorite color, which is purple. It was a generic, one-size-and-one-color-fits-all tag.

The next thing I heard was the vet and my human talking about whether I should be fixed. Fixed! I wasn't broken when I came in here; why on earth do I need to be fixed? When I returned to my house, I thoroughly checked myself over; sure enough, nothing was broken.

Several weeks later I was whisked off to the vet's clinic to be fixed. I could have told my human that nothing was broken, so why not save the gasoline and just head over to the park for a nice walk? I have always had a strong belief that if it ain't broke, don't fix it. Do the humans listen?

No! At least on this visit, the vet gave me anesthesia. However, when I woke up I had a lampshade on my head. 'Boy,' I remember thinking to myself, 'I must really be a party animal.' But no, come to find out, the vet had torn my beagle suit and, in an effort to cover this up, had stitched me back up and stuck this silly lampshade on my head. I have determined that there is only one redeemable quality or use for this lampshade. It should be put on my humans' heads to prevent them from looking at their phones all the time.

Now, I am sure you pups are wondering what can be done to stop this crazy behavior so you no longer have to return to the vet. Allow me to state for the record, I have it all figured out. I feel it is only fair to have each and every vet bill calculated in dog dollars. That's right, each dollar spent would equal seven human dollars. For example, a one hundred dollar vet bill would become seven hundred dollars. Once that is put into legislation and passed by Congress, trust me, our trips to the vet's office would be limited if not stopped altogether.

Howl-I-Days

AH, THE HOLIDAYS! NOTHING is quite as festive as our house around the holidays. Nonetheless, nothing is more confusing for us fur-kids than the holiday humans call Christmas. The first thing I notice around my household is my human's unusual spending patterns. The human will start making a series of random purchases and then hide them like the little brown squirrel out back stashes acorns for the winter. They think we fur-kids don't notice this, but I have caught my human hiding things under the beds, in the backs of closets, and in the trunk of the family car. The fact is, if they would allow me to help, I would be more than happy to dig an adequately large hole in the flowerbed that would more than accommodate this issue.

Shortly after they hide the presents, they can't remember where they hid them. Oh yes, more times than not I have found gifts stashed in and around the house several years after they were purchased. Trust me, our humans could never dig a hole in the backyard, hide a bone, and be able to find it ten seconds after they covered it up, let alone a day or several weeks later. It simply isn't in their DNA.

Next, they begin a ritual of bringing home colorful paper. I am not talking about a few sheets of paper, either, pups. We are talking about enough paper to stretch from the East Coast to the West and back again. Why do they need all this paper, you ask? Let me tell you. They begin wrapping the presents they have been lucky enough to find. This leads to overages in the paper department due to their inability to find the remaining presents they stashed away. Do they return the paper surplus and get some spare change to buy me extra kibble or treats? Of course not! My human, like all humans, can never return paper or ribbon. Instead, they take up a complete section of a closet with wrapping paper and bows, which they will never again use in a million years. Oh, one word of caution. Never, and I mean never, stand beside your human when they open that closet with the gift-wrapping supplies in it. I have witnessed many paper and bow avalanches in my lifetime. In fact, I am in the process of making a movie with the Discovery Channel about this very topic.

Next comes the most confusing part of this holiday for 99.9 % of all us fur-kids. Suddenly, without warning, a tree sprouts up inside the house! This tree has its very own water bowl. This is quite useful, I might add, as there is nothing more festive than having a drink underneath the Christmas tree. However, you should do this only when your humans are not around. They must have somehow noticed how tasty the water is underneath the tree and will chase you off. The next tree issue confuses my little beagle brother, Tyler, and I'm sure the vast majority of male canines. Unlike with the trees out back, the human does not allow him to lift his leg on this tree. I am undertaking an ongoing investigation to determine how the inside tree is any different from the outside trees.

If that isn't enough, next the humans in the household will pull out boxes and tubs and begin hanging things, including electrical lights, off the tree. As part of my extensive research, I recently interviewed a Labrador retriever who had chewed on one of the cords on the tree and was shocked. He now looks like a poodle. In fact, I think this may be how the poodle breed came about. If the human breed needs to light up this indoor tree, there should be a warning to first measure your fur-kids' tail height and then put the lights above that level.

I have had a string of those lights about a mile long follow me out from under the tree more times than I care to mention. However, does my human understand this? Let me tell you, they haven't a clue!

Next, trees were made for us canines to lie under. However, leave it to the human to mess up even that for us fur-kids. Your human will put their colorfully wrapped packages under the tree. While it is fun to unwrap each item, I do this for the sole purpose of ridding the household of the surplus paper and bows. Does my human appreciate this? No! Nevertheless, in the process, on several occasions I have found a few tasty treats in one or more of those packages.

I also have to warn all of you about the photo shoot under the tree. You'll know when this is about to happen, as every human in the household will surround the tree in matching sweaters and occasionally silly hats. Next, they will make you wear a matching sweater. The entire family, you included, sits on the floor and a series of blinding flashes goes off. After this ridiculous task is done, you will never see them wear those sweaters again. The human breed – go figure.

I have heard that Santa keeps some type of list, a database or spreadsheet that the little elves keep up to date. On this list are all the humans and, yes, even us fur-kids. It is divided into two sections: the naughty and the nice. However, I wish someone could define for us canines what exactly being naughty is. Regardless, I would like to say to Santa, I can explain!

On Christmas morning, once again everyone in the household gathers around the tree to open the presents under it. Oh, try to look excited when you get another collar. I have learned to perfect this technique by watching my human dad when he gets socks or a tie.

The next holiday that really chaps my hide is Thanksgiving. It is clearly the wrong name for this holiday, at least as far as we canines are concerned. You see, Thanksgiving is a holiday on which your human becomes the hunter and bags a rather large bird, then brings it home to cook. Nevertheless, the human fails in the area of pack-like rules, as the human does not share the food with the rest of the pack. The smells from this feast fill the house for the day. For this reason, I am petitioning Congress to change the name of Thanksgiving to Torment Your Dog Day.

It is very important to note that a cooked or uncooked bird left unattended on the table is an open invitation to any red-blooded canine to devour it! It doesn't seem fair that when the family sits down to eat a massive feast large enough to feed a Third World country, you are offered your usual bowl of kibble and a tiny slice of turkey. This is why I usually feast on the trashcan later.

The other human holiday that makes no sense at all is the 4th of July. This is when some humans spend twice the national debt on things they blow up…and I spend the night under the bed, shaking my beagle boots off from all the noise. I have also noticed that many humans do not get the memo that the 4th of July is one day long. Some humans think the 4th starts a month before and lingers for at least a month after.

Another human holiday that makes absolutely no sense at all is Easter. I am not sure how a rabbit appointed himself the national spokes-bunny for this holiday. I might add that there are millions of chocolate replicas of this furry little creature lining the shelves of a store near you. I am no farmer, I fully admit this, but don't eggs come from chickens? How in the world did this bunny hone in on the chicken in the first place? I know for a fact that chickens are working around the clock as we speak to produce eggs for this holiday – and all the while, that long-eared rabbit takes all the credit. I urge you and your human to contact Congress and request the impeachment of the Easter Bunny once and for all, then ask that the Easter Chicken be appointed as the holiday icon.

The fact is, if canines were put in charge of holidays, we would have such days as National Eat Pot Roast Day, Tummy Rub Day, and Never Take a Bath Day (which would last 365 days a year), to name just a few.

The Mystery in My House

MY HUMAN PARENTS HAVE no clue about the mystery that lives within the walls of our home. I truly believe Alfred Hitchcock, 20/20, or Dateline should have made a movie about this by now. If not, maybe I should put on my producer/director's hat and create a film of my own.

Allow me to explain. Mysterious things happen when my parents leave the house. I am sure you pups have had this same thing occur at your house. The human breed wonders why many of us suffer from what is deemed separation anxiety when it really has nothing at all to do with that. The fact is, it is the mystery we pups all face when our parents are not around. Once the door creaks shut, that is when a trashcan mysteriously falls over, or when a shoe or magazine gets chewed up. Mind you, I am innocently sleeping in my bed, as is my beagle brother, Tyler, or we are simply watching over the household like good canines do.

Then my parents come home and say, "Someone knocked over the flower vase in the living room!"

They assume that stance. You know, the one with their hands on their hips and disapproval on their faces as they look at both of us.

While I would like to blame it on my beagle brother, and many times have done so in the past, do you know who Someone is? I am sure each and every one of you is as clueless as I am about this person they call Someone. I can tell you for a fact that I am not familiar with Someone. I have never been introduced to anyone named Someone. However, what I do know – and this is from years of doing my own gumshoe (or I should say gumpaw?) detective work – is that there is, in fact, a Boogie Beagle alive and well among us. No matter what breed you are, you have a Boogie Beagle or Boogie Collie or…well, I am sure you understand, simply fill in your breed. In our situation, the Boogie Beagle comes alive when our parents leave the house, or sometimes at night when all of us are fast asleep. The Boogie Beagle is gutsy, too – don't kid yourself. Your parents can simply leave a room and that wicked monster will steal their sandwiches from the coffee table faster than you can say "The Boogie Beagle did it."

Who is this mysterious Boogie Beagle, you ask? Well, he is the beagle that knocks over the vase, shreds the magazines, chews the shoes, and knocks over the trash-can. In short, the Boogie Beagle lurks within the walls of our home and sometimes in the family car or backyard.

Depending on how evil the Boogie Beagle is in your house, things can get even worse. In fact, I know of a rottweiler that had a Boogie Rottweiler living with him and his parent. For years, the Boogie Rottweiler would pee on the carpet, chew the furniture, and dig up the backyard. There was simply no end to what this malicious, mischievous, spiteful Boogie Rottweiler would do. My friend the rottweiler had to finally hire an attorney from the law firm of Beagle, Bassett, and Schnauzer to represent him. The case is now before the grand jury. I myself have helped him by pitching in several thousand dollars for his legal fees. The poor thing has been going to a doggie therapist for years. I hope and pray that the private eye to whom my money has gone will someday expose the true identity of the Boogie pups that live among us and bring them to justice once and for all.

Adopted?

I AM STILL LOOKING into this matter. In fact, I have contacted several agencies that deal in issues like this. I looked for a birth certificate in the house. I found all types of papers with my name on them, and one said pedigree. Not sure what that was, and I am still wondering.

I have managed to collect DNA samples from both my human parents – without their knowledge, of course. I have also collected my own DNA and sent everything in for testing. I suggest all you pups do the same.

I never really questioned who I was until Petunia, that stupid cat next door, told me I was adopted. I think she may be a distant relative of the Boogie Cat.

Not that I think Petunia is an expert on the subject of heritage or anything as deep as DNA, and I am sure she is wrong. What does a cat know, anyway? She was the one that told me Santa Paws doesn't exist. I think that was because she was on the naughty list that year.

However, looking back, I can't really remember my birth. It is a complete blur. The furthest back I can remember is puppyhood, with the warm little bed and blankies and squeaky toys. There were endless photos with lots of flashing lights going off, too. It's a wonder I'm not permanently blind. I can remember the endless cooing, oohs, and ahs from my human mom and dad, not to mention when their friends came to visit me.

I have noticed that my parents seem to have some challenges walking on all fours like I do, unless I am under the bed or have knocked a toy under the couch. I just assume they are four-legged challenged. One observation I made was that we all have dark brown eyes. However, their coats seem to be lacking; probably that is the result of all the bathing they do.

Therefore, I just assume – once again, for the record – that the obnoxious cat next door is out of her furry little mind. Don't tell anyone, but on several occasions I have found her getting high on catnip. More than likely, she has some brain damage. Nevertheless, I have wonderful human parents. I wouldn't trade them for a million beagle cookies. No matter what the outcome is, I am a happy beagle. However, I will never tell Petunia she was right.

Speed Bump

MY HUMAN MOM AND dad have bestowed on me a nickname – "Speed Bump." I totally agree with you that it is not a very appealing name for an elegant beagle lady like myself. I am neither yellow nor black, nor do I lie across a street or parking lot to slow down cars.

Nevertheless, after careful observation on my part, I believe this rather inappropriate nickname was given to me because of my preference for lying across the doorways in my house. Pups, pay close attention here. If you do not already do this at home, you should. The human breed has a tendency to get up without warning and leave the area with not so much as a word to us. I truly believe humans are wanderers by nature. Off they go, into the next room, out of the house, into the backyard, or driving off in the family car.

We do not want to stifle their growth in terms of tracking abilities or finding their way back home without our help. God only knows they all seem challenged in their tracking skills – or lack thereof. Nevertheless, we must know where they are, as most of the time they have no idea themselves, even within the confines of the household.

Proper placement in the doorway is vital, and each canine in the home must plan strategically. Oh, I know your human will be upset about having to step over you or go around you. Do not let this deter you. Allow me to provide some enlightenment.

The kitchen is one doorway I love to lie across. Why, you may ask, is the kitchen so important? It is simple. This way I can get my beauty rest while keeping an eye on the activity in the kitchen and the all-important food inventory. If a human enters the kitchen and opens a cabinet door, pantry, or refrigerator, I can spring into action. I carefully place myself next to the human. Okay, it is not the human I am really interested in; it is the food. Closely watch the food as the human moves it around from the refrigerator to the countertop. Your human can make food disappear; I am not pulling your tail here. In fact, I have had several calls from Las Vegas wanting to book my human and their food act.

Anyway, back to what I was saying. Your placement under their feet is vital for watching the food. I would like to issue a warning here. Your humans will call this "getting under their feet." Trust me, each step we fur-kids take is strategically placed and planned. This is for optimal food recovery. Let's face it, humans are not very graceful at handling food in a kitchen.

The fact is, the speed-bump technique is part of the pack-like nature our ancestors figured out a billion years ago. Their goal was to guard the food supply. Thus, as you may have already guessed, the kitchen is one of the most important areas of any canine home. Therefore, you will often find me stretched across the doorway leading into the kitchen.

While I am on the subject of kitchens, I must mention an issue I have with the modern human homebuilder breed. It seems they are under the misconception that all homes need what is known as an open floor plan. This can allow for either two access doors into the kitchen or no doorways at all, just wide-open space. Open floor plan, my beagle butt! This is a nightmare for any canine. I simply cannot keep a close eye on the most vital area of the house with this design. Take note, human homebuilders: The ideal floor plan requires that the builder first measure the household canine. The doorway leading into the kitchen should not exceed the length of the canine. The same principle applies to the hallway leading to the front door of your house or the garage door, whichever your human leaves from. Again, this is vital for you to carefully monitor your humans when they slip their leashes and leave the house. You are aware they have left, and you can set your canine clock to track how long they are gone.

I have contacted my Congressmen to request the creation of a Human Pet Parent Alert, much like an Amber Alert or a Silver Alert for a missing child or senior. I think this is essential; when your human has not been seen for three hours (which is 21 hours in dog time), you can call in and report them missing. God knows, if we pups don't keep an eye out for our humans, who on earth will?

While I am on the subject of doorways, allow me to expand on the subject. There is yet another doorway we must watch over. That's right, it's a tough job we pups have but someone has to do it. Your human may call it the bathroom, the head, or the executive washroom. Don't even ask about how or why they would consider that last term. I am as clueless as you are. However, what I do is lie in the doorway or go into the bathroom with my human. Our humans just can't seem to wrap their brains around why we pups like to watch over them in this most dangerous room of the house. It is beyond me why any homebuilder must construct one or more of these rooms in every house they build. Duh, why don't our humans just do their business in the backyard, like we do? It is beyond me. My brother and I have been going out back for years, so why don't they? No, they prefer to do their business in that little room that scares the beagle boots right off me. It has that hose coming out of the wall that they wash me with. There is also a large white bowl of water with a handle that, when pushed, causes the water to swirl around like a vortex. It sounds as loud as a tornado warning.

My human – and I am sure yours as well – uses the bathroom. They would rather open the lid on that large water bowl they call a toilet and use that. Did you know it has a huge – I mean huge – hole in the bottom of it? It is about the size of the Grand Canyon! Your human could accidentally fall into it and never be seen again. God only knows how deep the hole is. Come to think of it, maybe I should invite over Petunia, the evil cat from next door. Hmm…you know, as curious as she is, I could tell her I wonder where that hole goes or maybe that I heard catnip was down there. As soon as she got into the bowl to inspect the situation, I could reach up and push that lever. Round and round she'd go and where she'd stop, nobody would know.

The Cold Beagle Shoulder

YES, EVEN A MILD-MANNERED, good-natured, sophisticated beagle like me gets upset with my humans from time to time. Once again, pups, you can fill in your breed here and give your human the cold bassett or cold foxhound shoulder. It works the same no matter what breed you are. Now, let's get down to business.

If you don't like something your human has done, you must show your disapproval, and I have found that the cold beagle shoulder is one of the best human training methods there is. How else can you train them, I ask? I have created seminars for training your human. If fact, I am sure it is only a matter of time before these seminars are offered all over the world.

First, let's talk about how long to carry this out. Duration is of the utmost importance in training your human. The fact is, they are usually clueless at first, so repetition is important.

For instance, when they insist on giving me a bath, for a minimum of one week I will give the cold beagle shoulder to the human who did this to me. If they take me to the vet, the duration of the cold beagle shoulder depends on what the vet person does to me. In this case, the time frame is anywhere from one to two weeks. If my humans are late with my dinner, no matter what their excuse is, it's a minimum of five hours.

Now that we have some guidelines for the time frame, the next thing to cover is how to properly execute the cold beagle shoulder for maximum effect. First and foremost, when the human talks to you, turn your back on him. Never – and I do mean never – make eye contact with them unless it is to give them what I call the stink eye. I'll explain that in more detail later. Your body language is vital for their training. How else will they understand that they have done something wrong? Remember, they are only humans.

Fur-kids, I do want to mention that proper use of the cold beagle shoulder can usually offer some benefits to us pups. That's right, shortly after you perform the first steps of the cold beagle shoulder, you can expect what I call "kiss-up treats" from your human. Enjoy them, as you have earned them. The next step is to expect more cuddling than usual. I know it will be very difficult to act like you are not enjoying this, especially if your human is good at cuddling. Act like you'd rather be having your nails done. Trust me, pups, this is all a part of the cold beagle shoulder routine. You may also expect more toys and food and also get to go bye-bye in the family car more often.

Lastly, as promised, the stink eye. I learned this technique from my humans. That's right, watch them when the male human forgets an important date. The female human will give the male the stink eye. Trust me, it is hard to miss. Again, the stink eye is very effective if you forget and do make eye contact with your human.

I Have a Voice I Simply Can't Control

MANY OF YOU HAVE already guessed that beagles, like me, just sound different. Some call it a howl, some a bay, but most beagle lovers – like my humans – say that beagles AR-ROOO. For those of you who have never had a beagle or lived next door to a beagle (or, for that matter, lived within a five-mile radius of a beagle), it can sound somewhat like a yodel. For this chapter, fur-kids, I wish this was an audio book so I could give you a really good example. While beagles do bark, when I get really excited, I AR-ROOO. Did you know that no matter what breed you are, you can ARROOO, too? My aunts, Chelsea and Brandy (both beagles, of course), lived next door to a doberman puppy. The poor pup was alone with no other fur-kids in his yard, so the little guy bonded with my beagle aunts. Chelsea and Brandy took him under their paws, per se. In no time at all, this little doberman was running around his yard ARROOOing like a beagle. Once the little puppy grew into a very large adult doberman, weighing in at a whopping 90 pounds, he was quite a sight to see. This huge doberman loped around his backyard, ARROOOing to protect it.

Anyway, back to what I was saying. My humans say I was born with the loudest ARROOO and bark they have ever heard. In fact, the way my human dad puts it, he feels as though people in the Third World can probably hear me. At this time, the

Noise Control Center, which is responsible for noise ratings in decibels, is still monitoring me to get a readout. However, I have shattered several meters in their failed attempts. What can I say? I have a great set of lungs.

I am really not sure how this happened. My biological sister, Penny, had an average ARROOO, and my brother, Tyler, has the tiniest ARROOO I have ever heard. Often, while in our backyard, I wanted so badly to play drill sergeant and say, "I can't hear you!" However, dignified lady that I am, I didn't. Most of the time I just laughed my beagle boots off when Tyler tried to ARROOO. I nicknamed him Squeaky Toy.

Trust me, when I ARROOO, I simply drown him out...but come to think of it, I can drown out passing freight trains miles away. In fact, I have offers from all the major railroad companies attempting to record my ARROOOing. If I accept these offers, just think; I'll be like Beagle Siri, voice of the railroads. One thing is for sure; the accident rate at railway crossings will decline, as my voice can be heard from miles away.

However, as stated above, I have a voice I simply can't control. My humans seem unable to wrap their brains around this fact. Take, for instance, a leaf blowing across the yard. I bark at it – and fur-kids, you should, too. We are what I like to term the "first responders" in our homes, in our yards, in our cars, and on our walks. If we don't issue an alert, who, I ask you, will? We must always be on alert to announce anything we see or hear.

Now, I will admit that I take issue with the black box in most living rooms called a TV. Nothing is more embarrassing than barking when the black box makes a doorbell sound, then taking off from a sound sleep toward the front door, barking at the top of my lungs while my humans laugh at me. I contacted all the network TV stations to file a complaint only to discover that this is simply an alert system to keep all us canines on our toes. Nevertheless, I have asked that each station insert a message for us stating that this is only an alert. Had this been an actual doorbell, someone would have been on the other side of the door. I have been told this message should be in place within a year or so.

For the most part, fur-kids, our humans are clueless as to why we bark. I think it has to do with how a human's brain is wired. Here's a good example. When was the last time you heard your human bark at the mailman or the UPS truck? I rest my case. Our humans simply do not understand the scope of alerting one another. Furthermore, there is nothing more distracting than when your human attempts to help. When I am barking at the top of my lungs and my human chimes in with their two cents trying to quiet me, all I hear is "blah, blah, blah." What I would like to say to them, if I had the time, is "Can you hold that thought? I'll get back to you. Can't you see I am extremely busy right now?"

Needless to say, here at our house we have surround sound. I'm the woofer and my beagle brother, Tyler, is the tweeter.

Baby Panda

Panda waiting for Santa Paws

Panda, Gunner and Daddy

Another Panda Pose

Panda's BFF Sadie

Just a typical day for Panda and Tyler
Tyler (Left) Panda (right)

Waiting for Thanksgiving

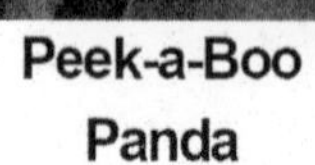

Peek-a-Boo Panda

Afternoon in Her Backyard

Patriotic Panda

That beagle never talks to me

Panda in her beagle buggy

Words I Don't Like

THERE ARE SOME WORDS I simply can't stand. I am sure you have heard some of them by now – or you will someday – and you dislike them as much as I do. Why humans always state these words in a louder-than-normal voice is beyond my highly intelligent understanding. Is there some unwritten law in the humans' handbook indicating that we canines have trouble hearing certain words? If they keep stating them so loudly, we will develop hearing problems. It reminds me of my human once talking to a person from Japan. My human dad was trying to ask about a product and he raised his voice. Did he think that raising his voice would somehow help the person understand the message better? Did raising his voice help translate the message into another language?

Anyway, let us take a look at the words. In the number one slot is "no."Your human usually states this in a very stern voice and sometimes uses actions as well. For example, humans may put both hands on their hips, displaying extremely hostile looks on their faces, and I do mean hostile. This is not the sort of look you normally see. Often, I do not even recognize my human when this occurs. I like to refer to this as a Jekyll-and-Hyde moment.

Another action with the word "no" is to point their index finger at something. Why they do this, I have never been sure. Take, for instance, when I was a puppy and I chewed up several pairs of my human mom's shoes. Honestly, I thought I was doing her a favor. Have you ever noticed the shape of those stupid things they stick their paws into on a daily basis? They look painful. They might as well go out into the garage and stick their feet into the vise on the shop table.

Anyway, she said "no" with a stern look like something out of a horror movie and pointed at all my hard work on her shoes. Did she think I didn't know what I had been doing for the last few hours was just for her benefit? No, she had to point at the shoes. Then she said, "Why did you chew only one of each pair?" Duh, did she have any idea how long this task took? No, she did not, nor did she care. Did she take into account the fact that I personally did not want her to ruin her paws in those things? Of course not. She was worried only about having a matched set of those vise grips to stick on her feet. Instead of giving me time to get to the other shoes so she did have a matched set with more room in each shoe, she put me outside. When the human says "no," I always want to say, "Why not?"

Next on my list are the words "stay" and "wait." Again, these are delivered in a stern voice. I want to say, "Hey, if you're going out the front door, why shouldn't I? Aren't we part of a pack, like a team? When was the last time you saw a football game in which the kicker kicked the ball, looked at his teammates and said, 'Wait,' or, 'Stay, I'll go do this myself?'" I rest my case.

The word "down" is another one I dislike. This is usually accompanied by the doorbell ringing. Once my human opens the door, I jump up on the visitors to greet them. After all, no one comes to see my humans. They come to see me, right?

The last word is actually a phrase: "that's all." This has to be the dumbest thing a human can ever say to their fur-kid. After I eat dinner with my humans, they look over at me and say, "That's all." Right, like I didn't see all that food in the pantry or the refrigerator when you opened it a few minutes ago. So, not only do humans think canines have a hearing problem, they must think we are blind, too.

Things Humans Waste Their Money On

SOMETHINGS IN MY household make no sense at all. I'm sure most of you fur-kids out there are just as clueless as I am about why our humans waste their hard-earned money on these things. Take, for instance, the thing that humans call a dishwasher. I could have bought myself at least a bazillion bags of kibble for what that metal noisemaker cost them. Not to mention those little packets of colorful food they feed that stupid machine. Allow me to explain. Any red-blooded canine is fully capable of prewashing those dishes. Furthermore, for a finishing touch, we'll give them a spit shine like you have never seen.

That's right, all of us fur-kids are pre-wired mentally and physically for the pre-wash and clean cycles. In fact, I have been in contact with many of the restaurants in my area to offer my services at a fraction of the cost of a dishwasher. The bonus is that I don't need those little packets of food they feed the dishwasher, nor do I use any electricity or water. That's correct, I need no electric outlet or water connection. I have a letter into Congress as we speak, requesting a rebate for any household or commercial business that uses a canine as a dishwasher. Think about it – we fur-kids are totally green.

Another benefit of using a canine for dishwashing is that no noise is associated with a canine washing your dishes. Have you ever heard some of those dishwashers? If not, you've probably been exposed to them in your own household way too long and are partially – or completely – deaf.

The other thing that chaps my hide is what the human calls a garbage disposal. Hello…your human, as well as mine, has a perfectly adequate disposal snuggled up right there at their feet, ready and willing to dispose of any food product they wish to toss our way. Am I right, fur-kids? Plus, an added benefit is that there are no worries of drain clogs like with the under-the-counter disposal, which sounds like the neighbor's cat when someone steps on her tail. Another benefit is that we don't need any of those little lemon drops the humans toss down the drain when the stupid thing has an odor. Now, that's not to say some food doesn't give us a little bad breath or gas, but that passes quickly (no pun intended).

Plus, as I'm sure most of you have figured out, there is zero cost to operate us. Again, no electricity, outlets, wiring, or water whatsoever.

Vacuum cleaners are the next thing I would like to discuss. My human – and, I'm sure, yours – has one of these things. Once again, it's a total waste of money as far as I'm concerned. Oh, vacuums come in a variety of fashionable colors and shapes. Some are bag-less, some require bags, and others are cordless or even remote controlled! However, we pups are much better than any vacuum cleaner on the market at picking up spillage or crumbs that land in our zone. "Why?" you may ask. It's as simple as the nose on your face.

In fact, that's why we're superior – our noses. That's correct, we can sniff out where the crumb landed or bounced. As far as spillage goes, no need for a special wet vacuum because we canines can handle any liquid, whether indoors or outdoors. In fact, we're so portable that we can clean up the family car. No extension cord or batteries are needed. Once again, another total waste of money by the human.

Next, let's discuss the topic of the home security system. With a canine in the house, there is no need for one. My research on this topic tells me that canines have been protecting the home since the era of cavemen. That's right, our canine ancestors constituted the first household security system. My great-great-great-great-grandfather was one of the first canines to protect the caveman. A quick look will reveal why we are more efficient than an alarm system. First, there is no need for a keypad with a code to remember. You don't have to set the alarm before you leave – no, just good old Fido on patrol. Also, there's no monthly fee to operate us. Furthermore, when the electricity goes out, the canine is

still 100% activated. I think you can clearly see how the humans are wasting OUR
money.

Things Humans Waste Their Time On

WHEN IT COMES TO wasting time, humans have cornered the market for sure. Case in point: I can be outside protecting the perimeter of the property while my human is inside staring like a zombie at that black box with pictures on it. This, my little furry friends, happens every evening until bedtime in my house, as well as in households across the world. I ask you, why don't they join us in the yard to sniff around and protect the house, roll in the grass, bark at a leaf blowing across the yard, or chase the neighbor's cat over the fence? At least these things would stimulate their senses. No, they would rather sit in this zombie-like state and turn their human minds into the consistency of a slushie.

Another baffling thing is what they call "going shopping." I fully understand the importance of going out to hunt and restock the kitchen with food, as well as to refill my kibble container and treat jar. However, more often than not, they come home with more human suits. Don't believe me? Check out their closets. They have things for their upper bodies as well as their lower parts. They even have things that go under all of the above, and at other times of the year, over everything. I'm still not sure why. Wasteful, I say! I have been wearing the same beagle onesie since I was born. I neither have the need to shop for a new beagle onesie nor to put things under it as the human does.

Some humans are so obsessed, it's as though they're addicted to this thing called shopping, either outside the house or online. I ask you, shouldn't one outfit last them a lifetime?

Another thing your human wastes time on is that tiny thing they carry in their pockets or that the lady human carries in the bag she carts around – the one that weighs as much as she does. They call it a cell phone. What makes it even worse is that some human, I'm not sure who, decided to create a smartphone. Trust me, pups, at any given time your human can be found staring at that thing. At one time, it used to ring, and your human could be heard barking back at someone. Not now, though, oh no. Now they just sit and stare at the thing.

Oh, it does have one redeeming quality – it takes pictures. However, even that has some issues. Take, for instance, when I sleep in an odd but very comfortable position. My humans must take a photo of it and post it on some place out there called the Internet. Now, I really don't mind them taking photos of an elegant pose that I strike. But, really, must they take and share with millions of people a photo of my head hanging off the couch and my lip dangling almost to the carpet? I have contacted the law office of Beagle, Basset, and Schnauzer, and they are looking into what we canines can do to protect our privacy.

Nonetheless, our humans waste 90 % of their time staring at that stupid phone. I mean smartphone. I say that humans should not be wasting time. They should be focusing their attention on us. We need more walks, playtime, and petting. Those should be their priorities!

Laundry Day

LAUNDRY DAY AT MY house consists of my human mom gathering up all the human suits she and my human dad wore throughout the week. She reminds me of that little brown squirrel gathering nuts in my backyard. I'm sure you're wondering: What is the reason for this? Again, I believe the reason is the human breed's obsession with being clean. Go figure. To me, this is so unnecessary.

Anyway, as I was saying, it's off to the laundry room with several arms full of what they call clothes. There, high on a shelf, are more bottles of smelly stuff than I can count on my four paws. If I stay in that room for more than five seconds, I come out smelling just like the flower garden out back.

Next, my human mom will create random piles of the clothes, putting them on the floor around the big white box. There must be some human logic to the piles, as on several occasions I have grabbed an item from one pile and carried it to another only to have her put it back in its original pile. Why? I can't seem to figure out the meaning behind the separate piles, though one thing I can tell you is that these piles make for fantastic, comfy beds. Curious to know how? Here's a step-by-step procedure for you to follow.

Step one: Pick a pile. Step two: Climb into the middle of that pile. Step three: Scrunch the pile with your front paws while turning around in a small circle. I like to call this step "nesting." Step four:

Lie down. If it doesn't feel quite right, simply get up, paw the pile while turning around, and lie down again. Once the pile is to your liking, fall asleep. Nothing is more appealing or calming than falling asleep surrounded by the scent of your human.

However, remember that you should never remove items and take them to another room. My little beagle brother, Tyler, liked to steal things and put them in random places around the house. I honestly think he was showing the early signs of becoming a Beagle Interior Decorator. Furthermore, if the doorbell rings, never, ever grab an item and bring it to the guest. One day, Tyler happened to greet a guest with a pair of underthings proudly displayed in his mouth. When my mom tried to grab it from him, Tyler interpreted this as a game of tug-of-war. 'Game on,' he thought. This was clearly not the case. The confusing thing is that the piles are clearly in the canine zone – on the floor. Why can't they be beds and toys? Suffice it to say, this upsets my human mom.

I'm still researching what the piles are, why she separates them, and why we dogs can't remove items before they go into the large, noisy contraption the humans call a washing machine. Oh, by the way, while we're on that topic – I can't be totally sure, but I think this machine is the littermate to the dishwasher in our kitchen. I have my staff digging into its ancestry at this time.

Once your human mom or dad puts a pile of clothing into the big white box, plug your ears, as this thing sounds like a jumbo jet. When it comes to the things that humans purchase and put into our homes, it seems their philosophy is "the noisier, the better." Oh, and when the machine comes to a stop, don't let your guard down. The stupid thing uses a loud buzzer to call out to your human. My human mom runs through the house and straight to the machine like the doorbell just rang. If I didn't hate the sound so much, I'd like one to call my humans when I want dinner or a treat.

Anyway, as I was saying, she then gathers those human suits out of the big white box. Next, she tosses them into the large box beside it. This is what they call a dryer. The magic happens here. While I'm not a fan of all the human suits my mom and dad have, I do love when the thing called "folding the clothes" happens. My human mom pulls each item, one by one, out of the dryer, puts it on the table, flattens it, and sets it in a large white laundry basket. Fur-kids, don't worry if your human has a basket that's another color; it's okay. We used to have a blue one until my beagle brother, Tyler, decided it was a toy.

Next, fur-kids, if you can, jump or step into the basket as soon as your human leaves the room. There, you'll find the warmest place on earth to nestle and sleep. That is, until the human comes back and finds you in the basket. I'm not really sure why this is so upsetting, as once I get out, I have always noticed that I have compressed the human suits and that my human mom can put a lot more into the basket. At any rate, make the most of your laundry day with your human.

Dressed Up

I AM NOT QUITE sure who decided we canines needed to play dress up but rest assured, it was a human. Trust me, I don't need any research or investigation to figure out this one. I fully admit that, from time to time, a beagle girl like myself enjoys wearing some bling around my neck in the form of a collar. For each month, I have a collar that is color-coordinated with the time of the year. Also, I have been known to wear a jingle-bell collar for the Christmas holidays, and I do have a few bandanas in my wardrobe. However, that's where I draw the line!

I was on my daily walk, quietly strolling around the block, when suddenly there it was. What the heck was it? I barked at the top of my lungs at whatever was walking toward me. I had to let the Third World know there was some kind of danger.

It was then that I saw what it was, but it was hard to believe my eyes. I knew that no one had spiked my water bowl. What was before me was my dear friend, Lola. Lola lives about four doors from my house. She is a purebred lhasa apso. Now, for the record, I would like to add that she has a more-than-adequate coat of fur for her lhasa apso suit. What caught my eye was the hot pink sundress. No, it wasn't on her human. It was on Lola. Her ensemble included a matching collar, a leash, a ribbon in her hair and booties. The booties made Lola walk as if she were an Arabian horse high stepping in a parade. Poor Lola was deeply embarrassed as my beagle brother and I approached her. One thing is for sure; I bet

Lola lost five pounds that day high stepping around our neighborhood. Poor thing. I hope when she got home she carefully put away that outfit. You know, somewhere safe like in a large hole in her backyard.

The next time I witnessed this crazy behavior was around Halloween – which, for the record, is not one of my favorite holidays unless I can snag some goodies from one of those tiny humans. Anyway, a few weeks before Halloween I accompanied my human to the pet store. Once inside, I noticed a woman sticking a helpless pug into a bumblebee costume. Yes, you heard me, a bumblebee! Can you believe that?

"Lady, if you wanted a pet bumble-bee, why didn't you just get one in the first place?"

I was hoping this dress-up thing was just a phase. But no, we canines could not be so lucky. The following year my human mom came home with a large hotdog bun.

At first, I thought she had supersized my dinner order. Let me tell you, I was ecstatic! If the bun was that big, can you just for a doggone minute picture the hotdog? I started to drool. That was, until I learned the hotdog was nowhere to be found and the bun was a fake. Oh yeah, and it got worse. She put that stupid bun on me and strapped it on! I was the hotdog inside the bun. She then stood back and grabbed her camera. Oh sure, humiliate me, why don't you? Let me first explain that if God wanted canines to roam the earth in dresses, t-shirts, hats and Harley jackets, we would not have been born with such beautiful coats of fur. Right, pups? Some things just need not be accessorized, and your canine is one of them.

Whose Bed Is It, Anyway?

THE NEXT TOPIC I would like to discuss is the bed. No, not the little one in the living room we use for napping. I'm talking about the large one in the master beagle bedroom. Remember, pups, simply insert your breed – if you're a poodle, it's a master poodle bedroom, and so on.

As I was saying, there seems to be some disconnect or lack of understanding between human and canine as to the ownership and occupancy of the bed. Allow me to state for the record that the large bed in the master beagle bedroom is ours! If you canines wish to allow your humans to sleep or nap with you in the bed, that's up to you.

Nonetheless, be sure to establish strict ground rules early on regarding where your humans are allowed to sleep. I bring this up only because a dear friend of mine, a little Boston terrier, found herself embroiled in a battle with her human over who belonged in the bed. I referred her to the prestigious law firm of Beagle, Basset, and Schnauzer. When the poor little Boston terrier had a simple gas problem, her human banned her from the bedroom and the bed! Why, you may ask, did the Boston terrier not lay down strict guidelines with her human as to the bed's ownership? If strict guidelines had been established, the human – and not the Boston terrier – would have had to seek other accommodations.

If you do allow your human to sleep in the bed with you, you'll find that space is another issue, though I simply don't understand why. To get comfy, we pups will change positions several times a night. Let's say my head is at the 12 o'clock position when I first go to sleep. Like most of you, I'll make my way around the clock throughout the night. This is what I refer to as "canine sprawl." For some reason, humans don't seem to understand how much space we canines require to accomplish these vital movements. For example, I overheard my human discussing her confusion over how a beagle 15 inches tall could take up so much space in the bed. Since I have allowed my human to share the bed with me, it would make things so much easier to simply draw a line from top to bottom showing the human where they are allowed to sleep. We canines require three-quarters of the bed, and the human can have one-quarter. I have contacted several brand-name sheet and blanket manufacturers to design a sheet and blanket for this purpose, with the lines clearly marked.

The next issue seems to be the pillows. I'll be the first to admit that I love putting my head on a soft pillow. However, have you fur-kids ever noticed just how possessive humans seem to be over pillows? Again, this is the risk any canine takes when allowing their human to share their bed. Like the bed, the pillows are the sole property of the canine. So, once again, strict rules must be established early on and reinforced with good training of the human. If that doesn't work, I say send them to the guest room to sleep.

Black Boxes

WHY DO I HATE black boxes so much…and what exactly are they? I am sure you have all heard about black boxes and how vital they are to an airplane. I am an advocate for those black boxes. Instead, the black boxes I am referring to have something to do with travel, and sometimes airplanes, but they are not an integral mechanical part of an airplane at all. The black boxes I am talking about are in almost every house. Check your human's closet. Trust me, humans have at least one black box, if not more, in their possession. In fact, they usually have a complete family of those stupid things in their closets or stashed in the garage. I think the black boxes reproduce wherever they're stored. Our humans call them suitcases. Fur-kids, heed my warning! And don't let down your guard if they enter your house in other colors, like red or purple. No matter what color they are, they're trouble.

I remember the first time my humans came home with one. I don't think it even wanted to enter our house, as my human had to drag it through the front door. Once it was inside, I sniffed it and then backed away, knowing it could only mean problems for my beagle brother and me! My human laid it on the floor and opened it. The poor thing had not eaten in weeks, maybe months, as the stomach area was completely empty – absolutely nothing was in there. My human mom started piling their clothes inside. Suddenly the box was stuffed. I assume it must survive on human clothes.

Lord knows humans have enough of those to feed an army of black boxes. It doesn't play with my toys, nor does it eat my kibble or try to steal a place in bed, so who cares, right?

WRONG! Once your human feeds their clothes to the stupid black box, it is stuffed and happy and off it goes. While you would think this isn't so bad, the black box actually takes your human along with it. I once called the police department to report the abduction of my humans. When asked for a description of the abductor, I described the stuffed black box. The police officer on the phone started laughing and then hung up on me.

On each occasion when the black box takes my human off with it, my beagle brother, Tyler, and I are sent away to doggie boarding school, or we get a doggie sitter. What kind of deal is this? Why can't we go? That stupid black box enters our lives for a day and the next thing I know we are the unwanted fur-kids, left abandoned – unless you call doggie boarding school or the clueless doggie sitter fun. Do you know how long it takes to train a sitter to do what we want?

When my humans first reappeared with the black box, they put it away in their closet and I breathed a sigh of relief. However, the following year, out came that stupid black box again. You will never believe it, but it had a baby! Really, right before my eyes! No kidding, and my human mom helped deliver it. I wouldn't believe it either, but I was sitting right there when my mom opened it and pulled another black box out of it. It looked just like the big black box – only a little smaller. Like before, my mom fed both of them the human clothes and off they went. Don't try sitting or sleeping on the black boxes to prevent your human from leaving; I have tried, and it simply does not work.

We fur-kids must unite. I am putting together a task force to combat those darn black boxes and prevent them from entering our households. They are nothing but trouble. However, if your house already has black boxes, like mine does, you must take matters into your own paws. First, go in your backyard and dig the largest hole you have ever dug in your life – the deeper, the better. Then drag all the black boxes to the hole. Don't worry about ripping them to shreds in the process, as this will make it easier to bury them. Toss those darn things into the hole and backfill the hole as quickly as possible.

I would like to add one last note here. If you are lucky enough to have a friendly black box and you are invited along each time the human breed takes off with the box, that is okay.

Canine Senses

AS CANINES, WE HAVE keen, laser-like senses, far superior to anything the human breed could ever dream of. Getting the human to understand this can be difficult, if not impossible. Okay, pups, sit and stay while I explain.

Let us start with our sense of smell. Many humans seem to want to disguise their own scent. I am not quite sure why, but rest assured I have my team of experts looking into it. I can only speculate that our humans are attempting to ward off prey through all the things they dab, spray, and drench themselves in. Take, for instance, the thing my human mom calls perfume and the thing my human dad calls aftershave. They don't realize just how powerful that smell is to us canines. I can walk 12 blocks from my house and still smell that stuff. I have asked Congress to look into those two potent smells and the damage they do to our ozone layer. I am sure there must be a connection and that all perfumes and aftershaves should be banned immediately. I personally invite Congress to visit my humans' bathroom to look over all the creams, lotions, and sprays. No doubt the bathroom would be red-tagged.

Next, let's talk about our sight. Again, our vision is far superior to that of our humans. I remember my great aunt, Chelsea, telling me that humans once believed canines could see only black and white. That is simply not true. Try to explain this to most humans; they are clueless. Why else would I prefer all shades of purple collars while my brother's signature color is blue? Memo to all humans: Duh, we can see colors! The only way I got this across to my humans was to dig a hole in the flowerbed and bury any hues that were not in the purple color family. The exception to this was the time my human dad purchased the most adorable tiger print collar. Let me tell you, when I wore that, I was one hot hunka-hunka beagle burning love and every male pup in my neighborhood knew it!

My favorite thing is night sight. As you probably know, the human breed can't see squat at night. That is why they illuminate everything inside and outside the house. Even the refrigerator has a light. Give me a break; open that refrigerator door at 1 a.m. without the aid of a light and I can pick out a steak over goat's milk ten times out of ten. We also see things humans simply cannot – but more on that later.

Hearing is another sense in which we canines surpass the human breed. How many times has your human asked you what you are barking at? I am sure, like me, you give them a look of "What do you think I'm barking at and why aren't you barking with me?" A canine can hear up to a quarter of a mile away. Better yet, we can be sound asleep three rooms away, hear a cheese wrapper in the kitchen, and be there in a split second.

So, as you see, we canines far surpass the human breed in all the senses. It is no wonder they have come to live with us. How else could they function?

Things That Go Bump in the Night

AS I MENTIONED EARLIER in my chapter about sight, I promised I would discuss the topic of things only we canines can see. To be painfully honest, even felines like Petunia, that darn cat next door, can see things no one else can see.

Allow me to explain. I will never forget the passing of my oldest beagle brother, Gunner. Several days after his passing, I walked into my living room to sit on my love seat. It just so happens to be one of my favorite spots to sit and look out the front window. I can catch some rays if the sun is out, and bark at leaves as they blow across my front lawn. It was then that I saw Gunner sitting on the love seat. I turned and got the heck out of Dodge, as fast as my little beagle legs could carry me.

Nonetheless, my beagle mind kept wondering if I had really seen what I thought I had seen, or if those scraps of pizza crust I had eaten out of the trash earlier were making me hallucinate. So, I slowly slunk back into the living room. Sure enough, there he was, sporting wings and with a glow surrounding him. I barked at him to see if he would bark back. It was then that my human dad came into the room. He saw me barking at the love seat and he shook his head.

"What in the world are you barking at?" he asked.

What am I barking at? You're looking

right at him and you're asking me what I'm barking at.

He turned and walked away.

I barked louder. My human dad never seemed to notice that Gunner had returned and was sitting right there in front of him on the love seat. It was then that I realized we, as canines, have special abilities to see things no one else can see. From that point on, Gunner became a frequent visitor at our house. My guess is that he did this to check on all of us.

My favorite Gunner visit went like this. Gunner, mastering his angel talents, walked to the back door and scratched it. That was his signal that he needed to go outside and go potty. He taught all of us other beagles to do this, too.

My humans were watching TV in the den when my human dad got up without thinking and opened the back door. When he looked down, he realized no beagle was there. I was lying in my beagle bed along with my beagle siblings, Tyler and Penny. I almost busted my beagle gut laughing as he asked my human mom if she had heard the scratching at the back door. Yes, she replied. While my humans could not see Gunner, they could hear him. My humans seem to like when Gunner visits; it comforts them.

Now, I'm sure you think it is just other canines we can see. Not true. Shortly after Gunner passed away, my human grandfather, Frank, passed away as well. He visited us, as did my human dad's mom. Things like this are simply commonplace for us. Humans can't see what we can see; that is simply a fact. No amount of training can help them in this area. This is why the human breed is so dependent on us.

The Walk

THERE IS NOTHING QUITE as amusing to me as hearing my humans talking about walking us fur-kids. First and foremost, we are the ones who take them for a walk. Simple logistics can explain this. Think about it; who is in the lead most of the time? We are. You may walk beside your humans, but even with that, we are still a few steps ahead. Therefore, to set the record straight, it is the canine who takes the human for the walk. A simple pack-like chain of command can explain this. I have my team of experts working on an organizational chart to explain this to every human.

As canines, we fully understand pack-like behavior. There is always an alpha female and an alpha male in the pack. This dates back to our ancient ancestors. In short, there are leaders and there are followers. We canines – not the humans – are the leaders in our packs.

I am sure you are all wondering why some of us fur-kids are tethered to our humans with what is called a leash. Allow me to explain the reason why some humans prefer this. The leash is for the benefit of the human. As we discussed in earlier chapters, humans cannot track. They simply cannot pick up their own scent, much less another's, to find their way around. Therefore, they go to specialty stores or online and purchase high-priced leashes for themselves. My humans have several, in colors from lavender to deep purple, that they attach to me. My sister, Penny, has all shades of pink and Tyler, you guessed it, has all shades of blue. This is so we canines can take them for a walk and get them back to our house. There is a billion-dollar industry out there for canine products – including harnesses, collars, and leashes – that attach us to our humans. It's a total waste of money, if you ask me. However, I do need to mention that the boxes in which the store ships the products are great toys. Lastly, another thing I have found fun to do is wrap the leash around my humans' legs and take off running, spinning them like a top!

Anyway, back to what I was saying. If humans would simply adhere to the pack rules and follow us, every home with a canine could save hundreds, if not thousands, of dollars per year.

I suggest you do as I do: Teach your humans to pick up their scent. I have to say, this is not an easy task, like teaching a horse to do the tango. First, I understand that all humans are challenged because they insist on walking on their hind legs. Plus, they have a total lack of understanding of what we do while on a walk. Another human issue you will need to address is the fact that most humans require us to walk in a perfectly straight line. When tracking, that simply does not work. The next item you need to address with your human is the fact that they want to rush you when you are sniffing out a scent. There are simply so many smells – a literal smorgasbord – and so little time.

Your humans also have no clue about our social media. Take, for instance, a poodle, rottweiler, or another breed that left me P-mail. I do not read poodle, but I can decrypt the message. However, it takes time even for a master like me. Furthermore, if a mixed breed leaves a message, it may start as one dialect, then change mid-way into that of another breed. I almost need to be a canine linguistics expert.

As you may have guessed, there is also Poop mail. This is P-mail with an attachment. I have to unzip the file to get the gist of what the message is saying. Lastly, the neighborhood cats leave a lot of spam I have to weed through. Does my human get on all fours to learn to read it, or at a minimum do they bend down? No! My humans just walk past important messages each and every day. I am sure yours do, too.

I tell you, it is a wonder the human breed can even find its way around the inside of our home. A pup has to wonder what on earth they did before we came along to help them with tasks like leaving the house. I think that is why most homes have backyard fences. This way, humans can venture into the great outdoors without the aid of a leash and still find their way around and back home. I knew one Labrador whose house did not have a backyard fence. He told me his humans walked out the back door and were gone for weeks.

Lastly, when taking your human for a walk, note that most other humans will know your name, though very seldom will they know your human's name. I think this is because we are all so adorable; that is why we get so much attention.

That Does It, I'm Going to Grandma's

MY MOTTO HAS ALWAYS been "What happens at Grandma's stays at Grandma's." Many of you fur-kids may have one or two grandmas and grandpas, or even more. I have a good friend, a doberman, who has four grandmas, four grandpas, and four human dads. My guess is, his mom sent the other dads to the dad rescue to find them all new homes. It seems to me his human mom was doing a lot of shopping around for just the right husband or whatever humans do with their partners.

Anyway, back to what I was saying. For the record, allow me to state that I love my grandparents when they come to visit my house or when I go to theirs. Not that I don't love my human parents. Don't get me wrong, I do. But let's face it, fur-kids, your grandparents are nonstop fun, treats, belly rubs, cuddling, car rides, and petting. Let's look at some reasons why.

My human mom and dad can be a little too restrictive for my taste, and I'm sure yours can be as well, especially when it comes to a delivery system of treats or letting you do whatever you please. Consider this example. My human mom gives me one treat from a newly opened bag. I can clearly see the bag is full. I stand there and refuse to move, waiting for the next treat to be delivered or fall into the pup zone. Does she do that? No! She zips up the top of the bag and says, "That's all."

What do you mean "that's all?" I'm not blind. Next comes my favorite human behavior. She sets the bag down and holds out her hands, palms up like a poker player or magician, showing me that she has nothing in them. I have to wonder, 'What does she think, we're in Las Vegas and she has to show me there are no cards left? Or that this is a magic show and there's nothing up her sleeve?' I feel like saying, "Watch my trick, Mom. Put that bag of treats on the floor and allow me, your magic assistant, to make them disappear right before your eyes – and my paws will never leave the floor."

Another excuse is when she tells me, "Just one treat, you need to watch your weight."

Weight? Mom, I'm a beagle. I don't plan to walk the red carpet or model on a runway any time soon. Just give me more treats.

So, I stand there, and my mouth begins to water. We all know what happens when our mouths start watering. Drool happens. There's nothing I hate more than drool. I'm a distinguished lady, for goodness sake, but there's only so much my salivary glands can take. So, there I am, standing with a puddle of drool at my paws. To boot, drool hangs from my lips like two shoestrings on both sides of my mouth. Sometimes I wish I could will my drool to swing around like my good old buddy Harrison Ford did as Indiana Jones. You know, in the movie when his whip became an extension of his arm, reaching for anything he wanted. If I could do that, those treats would be mine in a heartbeat!

For that matter, there would be no kitchen counter too high for me to reach unattended food. Not to mention the refrigerator door; I could just swing my drool around the handle, open the door, and get what I wanted, when I wanted it. But no, drool is just that – plain and simple slimy goo dangling from my mouth.

As I was saying, grandmas and grandpas (and even aunts and uncles) are a wonderful delivery system for treats, fun, tummy rubs, and more. Also, they are much more generous in the treat department and so much easier to train to give you what you want. If Grandma is at my house, I have learned that if Mom says no, Grandma will say yes!

Even walks are handled differently. Your human mom and dad walk much faster. For instance, if I pick up a scent and want to sniff, my human parents will hurry me along. My grandma, grandpa, aunts, or uncles will allow me to sniff thoroughly until I am finished. I have my research team looking into the mystery of why this happens. Also, have you ever noticed that your grandparents' house usually has a complete shrine devoted to photos of their fur-kids at all ages? The other day, I was at the bank drive-through with my grandma. When the teller made a fuss over me and handed me a treat through the magic window, Grandma pulled from her wallet at least a billion photos of all her grand fur-kids.

I assume the true canine understanding must miss a generation. In short, Grandma is like Mom – only cooler! Nonetheless, I still feel that with enough training and patience, we can get our human parents up to our grandparents' speed. However, until that happens, I have Grandma JoAnne on speed dial.

How Not to Take a Pill

I, FOR ONE, HAVE never been a fan of taking medication. I think it's actually a maneuver on someone's part to make money off me while tormenting me in the process. When I was just a pup, I was prescribed a pill that was about the size of the garden tub in the master bathroom – I kid you not. My human mom was told to stick it in the side of my mouth with her finger and then down my throat. OMG, after my gag reflex stopped kicking in, I was able to simply deposit the pill back on the floor.

However, I quickly learned that this method of avoiding pills did not work. Take my advice, fur-kids, if your human parents attempt this insane method, happily keep the pill in your mouth, trot away, and find the nearest place to hide it. One word of caution, though; don't take too long, as I think that guy by the name of Frankenstein must work for all the pill companies. That's because all pills taste the same – awful! Once the pill starts dissolving in your mouth, it will taste like you've been licking a car tire for a week straight. Trust me, no amount of water from your bowl will get rid of it, either. The taste will last for at least two weeks.

Therefore, I use the drop-and-bury method. I take the pill to the closest thing I can find, like my mom's shoe or behind her pillow. After she has forgotten about it, I pick up the pill, take it outside, and bury it. Another word of caution: Do not bury it in your lawn, as I have found that most pills will kill the grass. They are simply not fit for your grass – let alone you – to take.

Next, I want to discuss the cheese or hotdog trick. It won't take long for your parents to figure out that sticking their finger and the pill in the side of your mouth isn't working. Next, they will try to disguise that nasty-tasting, torpedo-sized pill. Oh yes, sometimes they'll try cheese, a hotdog, lunchmeat, you name it.

This is one of my more desired methods. Why, you may ask? With a little practice, you can master the tongue-twist technique. Listen up, fur-kids. First, if you notice Mom or Dad lingering around the kitchen counter at a time when it's unusual for them to do so, this could be a red flag. Look for one of the brown or white plastic bottles where those stupid pills live and breed on the kitchen counter. Your parents are attempting to slip that huge pill into a ball of cheese or a hotdog so you'll take it while thinking you're getting a great-tasting treat. Not so fast, grasshopper! What you need to do is take the pill ball, then work your tongue to open and separate the pill from the treat. Be sure you don't swallow the pill; swallow only the treat. Walk away quickly and hide the pill. I'm sure that with practice, you, too, will become a tongue-twist master like I am. All the while, you'll look like you are simply enjoying the most wonderful treat on earth!

My Name is "Stop It" and His is "No, No"

IN AN EARLIER CHAPTER, I talked about how there should be some type of naming convention or standard imposed on humans when naming their fur-kids. Another vital issue plagues the naming of us canines across the world. Not to worry, as I have put it before Congress to look into.

Allow me to explain this perplexing dilemma. Many of us poor pups face confusion from the time we are wee babies. We receive nicknames and confusing commands that we mistakenly think are our names, but they aren't. To thoroughly understand this issue, we must go back to puppyhood. That's correct, way back to our beginning, when we were still learning what our human parents were attempting to say to us. Let's face it; the human language is lacking, to say the least. The Oxford English Dictionary contains a mere 171,476 words, and that is for only the English language. Many of us pups come from other countries. Simply put, human language is not as sophisticated as our canine language is.

Allow me to give you a personal example, if I may. As a very young pup, I thought for months that my name was "Stop It" and that my little brother, Tyler's, name was "No, No." This is why when our humans called out our real names (Panda and Tyler), we never went to them. For months, we had no clue who the heck Panda and Tyler were or why our human parents were calling their names.

It took us several months to understand that Stop It and No, No weren't our real names. Rather, these were commands our humans were giving us. I know this is a problem not only in our family but in others as well. I have a dear friend, a little Boston terrier. At the age of nine, the poor little fellow still thinks his name is "Bad Dog." I discovered this when I was out walking with my human dad and we came upon the terrier's human mom. She said his name was Rochester. While I fully understand that Rochester is quite a mouthful for a little Boston terrier, he really had no clue that his name wasn't Bad Dog. I tried to explain this to him countless times. Nonetheless, to this day I cannot get him to understand. Also, there is an English bulldog who thinks her name is "Quiet" and a schnauzer who thinks his name is "Enough." I hope you can see how humans give us pups very mixed signals.

This is an issue being worked on as we speak. I hope in time that the legislature will pass a bill requiring our humans to address us only by our real names. Thus, pets around the world will know who they really are once and for all.

The other thing we pups have a problem wrapping our brains around is the tone of our humans' voices when they talk to us. Have you ever noticed the changes? One minute their voices sound like baby talk, and the next they sound like Vincent Price in a horror flick as they yell commands at us. Now, I'll be the first to admit that when I see a cat cross my yard, my bark can be pretty bodacious. Never once, however, has it changed into something sounding like Cujo.

Lastly, I have an issue with nicknames. My humans say that nicknames are terms of endearment for us pups. However, many times this, too, can be very confusing. Take, for instance, this scenario. Tyler, my sister, Penny, and I are in the backyard and my human calls out, "You in the beagle suit." We all look up, as last time I checked, we all had our beagle suits on. Or "Wiggle Butt." It is a known fact that most of us canines wiggle our butts when we wag our tails. We finally figured out that nickname was given to my brother, Tyler.

My hope is to establish a school-like environment our humans can attend before they get a pup so they can learn good canine communication skills. In the meantime, listen to all that your humans are saying. If you hear them calling a name over and over, chances are that it is, in fact, your name.

Oh Sure, Post That on the Internet

IF THERE'S ONE THING that rubs my fur the wrong way, it's when one or both of my humans post something about me on one of the many social media sites on the Internet. I ask you, isn't there such a thing as privacy for us fur-kids? For heaven's sake, once, when we moved and changed vets, the old vet made my dad get on the phone before they would release my medical records to the new vet. So why, I ask you, is it okay to share questionable photos and say things about me on the

Internet, where anyone and their uncle can see this information? This is just not right! I'm a firm believer in the Pet Privacy Act, which I personally put together line by line. This bill is in the Senate right now. I hope it passes ASAP!

Fur-kids, we are all responsible for keeping a close eye on our humans' activities while they are on the Internet. I'm in the process of working with some of the most popular web browsers and their engineers to create a new browser with canine controls. This way, we can block any questionable activities by our humans with the flick of a switch. For those of you who have no clue why we fur-kids need a computer browser like this, let me give you a few examples.

When we lived in a two-story house, I tore the ACL in my knee while charging down our stairs. Mind you, it was urgent that I get to our front window to bark at the UPS man. I went through an excruciating surgery to have my knee repaired. Once home, I lay in my bed with my beagle suit shaved up to my stomach and on some drug patch called morphine (which, I might add, made my eyes feel like they were swimming in my eye sockets). I was so out of it for days, my human dad had to feed me chicken broth with a syringe. A beagle refusing to eat – I know...unthinkable!

Now, one would think a fur-kid would have her privacy during such a trying time, right? Oh no, my human mom took a photo and posted it on social media. When I finally recovered, which took about 1,500 dog years, I saw myself on the Internet and was simply appalled.

Another time, as I was walking by it, our trash just happened to tip over on me for no reason at all. Once again, another photo op, this time with spaghetti dangling from my beagle ears and sauce all over my face. My human dad grabbed his camera and quickly posted a picture on the Internet. If that wasn't enough, I once got my head stuck between the wooden spindles on the staircase. So, there I was, stuck. What did my human mom do? She took one look at me and started laughing.

"Oh sure, don't help me. Grab your camera and take a picture first."

Sure enough, my photo was posted on the Internet within seconds of her helping me from between the wooden spindles.

I know of several fur-kids whose humans made cardboard signs and hung them around their dogs' necks for photos with sayings such as: "I ate all the cat's food," "I'm a bad dog, I opened the door myself and got out when the doggie sitter was here," "I hid a raw steak in the couch," and "I chewed through the water meter and somehow flooded our yard." Public humiliation is what I call it.

Let's face it; with a camera and a connection to the Internet, our humans become paparazzi. We aren't safe even in our own homes, as you can clearly see.

One word of advice: Don't try to solve this problem by chewing up your humans' smartphones. Trust me, been there and done that! That thing has no taste, and someone at NASA must have designed the plastic. I gave up after about three hours of non-stop gnawing.

Nonetheless, make sure you get in your vote on the Pet Privacy Act. This is the only way we fur-kids can get privacy in our homes.

Rescue Me

OUR HUMANS DO A lot of silly things, as I've discussed in this book. However, once in a while they do some good and important things. I'm talking about our rescue friends. No guide on training your human would be complete without a chapter on this topic.

I myself was not a rescue. My human didn't know about such groups until long after my sister, Penny, and I came along. Nevertheless, my human dad rescued a small beagle pup when he was just a young pup himself. My dad jumped out of his truck during morning rush-hour traffic and scooped up a tiny beagle puppy. He named him Toby. Years later, my human mom and dad together rescued several others, and also fostered a few.

I myself have attended several rescue events with my human parents. My human dad is a writer, so I tag along to paw his books. Quite frankly, I help him write all those books and cartoons. Without me, I don't think he would be able to do it.

Anyway, as I was saying, rescue pups, if you are reading my guide, this is your first step to getting a forever home. Most rescues I have talked to think they have to wait around until a human decides to adopt them. Not true. First, it is the canine that adopts the human. Never forget that. Once you realize who rescues whom, you are one step closer to getting rescued.

Let's take, for example, the last rescue event I attended. Just before the event started, I had a heart-to-heart talk with a basset that was up for adoption. The poor little basset was a basket case, wanting so badly to have a home to call her own. After our talk, she was ready to find her human to adopt. I stepped aside as several people passed by. Suddenly, Jessie, the basset, spotted just the person she wanted to adopt as the lady stopped by her crate.

I had told the basset that step one was to get someone's attention, as there are usually many pups up for adoption at these events. My basset friend stood up and batted her big brown eyes at the woman. This got the lady's attention. Next, when the woman put her hand into the crate, Jessie licked it. Once you find your human, it's very important to take every opportunity to make physical and eye contact. This worked like a charm.

Next, the lady asked if she could pick up the basset. Jessie followed this by cuddling close to the lady. I witnessed the lady literally melting, cooing and talking baby talk to Jessie the basset. BINGO! My plan worked! Clearly, this lady – not my basset friend – was the one being rescued. Jessie was adopted and finally has a loving forever home.

I'll be the first pup to admit that choosing the right human to rescue is of utmost importance. Between you and me, some humans should never have a dog or cat – or, for that matter, even a stuffed toy likeness of one of us. Many of us fur-kids take for granted that we get our meals every day, a clean water bowl to drink from, a human we can walk with, and a nice, warm bed to sleep in. Many not-so-lucky pups and cats are dumped, neglected, or forgotten. Despicable, I say. As fur-kids, we understand only unconditional love, and we assume all humans will return this love and devotion. However, not all humans are the same. For this reason, it is vital that we pups choose the perfect human companion. We also have to help our humans give back to rescue groups so fur-kids like my new friend, Jessie, find great forever homes. I would also like to see a database of bad humans who abuse and neglect pets, so these humans will never be allowed to have another pet.

The Bridge

EVERY GOOD STORY HAS a beginning, middle, and end. I can't stress enough how important this chapter is. It discusses teaching your human about what is called the Bridge. As with everything and everyone, our time here on earth is simply not long enough. Nevertheless, there is a place we fur-kids know as the Bridge. Our humans, God love them, know that every human and pet simply can't stay forever, but with knowledge of the heart, we can make our passing a little easier on them. I myself started dictating this book while I was still on earth. However, the burden of almost 17 years in my earthly body became heavy before my human dad could finish writing. If you want to know the truth, I think he just couldn't type fast enough to keep up with me. Don't mention that to him, though. Being a good human dad, he promised to finish this book, but simply set it aside after I passed away on September 15, 2013. My dad found it too difficult to deal with the book at that time.

This book would never have been completed had I not kept pestering him to finish this most important work for me. Oh yes, we pups can still nudge our humans from the Bridge. In fact, I do it all the time. Listen up, so you can also train your humans to understand.

We fur-kids have little to bequeath to our loved ones after our passing from this realm of life to beyond. Nor do we waste our precious time on earth stockpiling things. Well, let's be honest; I may have left a bone or two buried in the backyard along with some toys in the neighbor's flowerbed and a few things under the couch. However, truly, the most important thing I left was my love for my human dad and mom, which they will carry in their hearts until I meet them at the Bridge. You see, we fur-kids don't want our human parents, family, and friends to grieve for us too long. When I was on earth, I wanted to bring joy, happiness, and smiles to them and everyone I met – never sorrow or hardening of their hearts. It gave me such heartache to see them hurt, and I'm sure other pups feel the same way about their families. I can truly tell you that I'm still with them even today, though not in the earthly body they came to know – and that is why they think I'm gone. Fur-kids, we must all work on our human parents to make them understand that the love we feel lasts an eternity and is not simply lost once we leave this earth. I hear them when they speak about me and I hear them when they are alone and talk only to me just as before. I'm also by their side when every tear falls.

One last thing, fur-kids – and this is the fun part for us. All too often, after losing a beloved fur-child, humans think they will never again be a pet parent. You can guide them to the canine you know will help them. I love my human parents beyond words that I can express. Simply put, it is unconditional. Fur-children know nothing about jealousy. We all want what is the very best for our humans and even our canine siblings left behind. Therefore, I set out on the most important search of my life – to find another beagle to fill the void I left behind. That's when I found a little 13-inch female beagle named Sundae. She has a lot of my traits and also my sister, Penny's, too. I used to always go into my human dad's office to help him with his writing and drawing. Sundae does the same thing. This doesn't mean for one second that I no longer love my human parents. It gives me a big beagle smile to see them laugh and play with Sundae. Oh, and by the way, if you're wondering, the Bridge is wonderful. I'm no longer in pain; I run and play with everyone up here as we wait for the ones we love. So, until we meet again, ARROOO and train your humans well.

About the Author

Timothy Glass was born in Pennsylvania

but grew up in Central New Mexico. He graduated from the University of New Mexico, and later spent some time in New England and central Florida.

Glass is an award-winning author, illustrator, cartoonist, and writing instructor. He has worked as a ghostwriter and story consultant. Glass started his writing career as a journalist under the pen name of C. Stewart. He has written and published more than 300 nonfiction articles nationally and internationally for the health and fitness industry. Glass worked as a regular contributing writer for several New York-based magazines. He enjoys the company of his wife, Cathy, and his tri-colored beagles. Glass is a member of the Author's Guild of America, the Author's League of America, and the Dog Writers Association of America.

Visit Us on the Web

Visit Tim's website at www.timglass.com. Also, don't forget to check out his beagle cartoons at http://www.timglass.com/Cartoons/

Join Tim on his fan pages:

Facebook: https://www.facebook.com/pages/Timothy-Glass/146746625258?ref=ts

Twitter: www.twitter.com/timothyglass/

LinkedIn: http://www.linkedin.com/in/timothyglass

Check out our Sleepytown Beagles fabric and wrapping paper:

https://www.spoonflower.com/profiles/sleepytown_beagles

A Message from Tim

I hope you have enjoyed this book, and there are more to follow. Book reviews are crucial, both for me as the author and for your fellow readers. Please take the time to leave a review at your favorite bookseller. I would greatly appreciate it.

Thank you,

Timothy Glass

Lightning Source UK Ltd.
Milton Keynes UK
UKOW01f0645280218
318620UK00001B/7/P